Jessica Jacobs Did
WHAT?

written by Nancy Ellen Hird
pictures by Andy Stiles

STANDARD
PUBLISHING
Cincinnati, Ohio

YE

The Standard Publishing Company, Cincinnati, Ohio
A division of Standex International Corporation
© 1994 by The Standard Publishing Company
All rights reserved.
Printed in the United States of America.
01 00 99 98 97 96 95 94   5 4 3 2 1

Library of Congress Catalog Card Number 94-2101
ISBN 0-7847-0180-6
Cataloging-in-Publication data available

Edited by Diane Stortz
Designed by Coleen Davis

Contents

Chapter 1

Jessica Jacobs turned her head
sharply to the clock
on the classroom wall.

"The bus for the field trip

leaves in five minutes," she said.

"Your mom will get here,"

said Sam.

Jessica tried to smile.

Sam and all the other

third graders

got up to leave for the bus.

5

Jessica's mother poked her head

into the room.

"Whew!" said Jessica.

She jumped up.

6

"Here is your permission slip,"
said Mrs. Jacobs.

"Now I can go," said Jessica.

"Thanks, Mom, for bringing it."

She zipped up her coat.

"And," said Mrs. Jacobs,

"here is your lunch."

"I forgot that, too?" asked Jessica.

Mrs. Jacobs rolled her eyes.

"Yes, and this is the third time

this week," she said.

"I think you would

forget your head

if it were not on your neck."

Jessica giggled
and touched her head.
"It's still there," she said.
"So far," said her mother
with a smile.

Jessica kissed her mother

and ran to the waiting bus.

She got in line

behind her friend Sam.

"I got it!" Jessica said.

She waved her permission slip.

"Great," said Sam.

"Was your mom mad?"

"No," said Jessica, "but I hope

I don't forget anything else."

"Did you ask her

if you can come

to my party tomorrow night?"

"Oops," said Jessica.

She pulled the invitation

from the pocket of her jeans.

"I forgot."

Chapter 2

Ring! R-r-ring!

The next morning,

Jessica reached out and shut off

her alarm clock.

Slowly she walked

to the bathroom.

She turned on the water.

She looked in the mirror.

She saw her blue nightgown.

She saw her neck.

But on top of her neck

there was . . .

The mirror is just

fogged up, thought Jessica.

She rubbed the mirror

with her hand.

Jessica looked in the mirror again.

Oh, no! she thought.

Where is my head?

And if I don't have a head,

how can I still see and hear?

There was a knock on the door.

"Jessica," called Mrs. Jacobs,

"don't let the water run."

Jessica turned off the water.

She did not want

her mother to come in.

She did not want

her mother

to see her like this.

Jessica wondered what to do.

Well, she thought,

I guess I don't

have to wash my face!

Chapter 3

Jessica opened the bathroom door.

She peeked out.

She heard bowls clinking.

Good, she thought.

Mom is in the kitchen.

Jessica ran to her room

and closed the door behind her.

My head must be here someplace,

thought Jessica.

She looked under the bed.

She found a sock,

a math paper,

a missing library book,

and her sunglasses,

but no head.

She looked in her closet.

But still she did not find

her head.

What am I going to do?

she wondered.

I have to go to school.

Jessica put on jeans

and a sweater.

She wrapped a long scarf

up and over her neck.

She put a big floppy hat on top.

She stuck her sunglasses

into the scarf.

Maybe, she thought,

no one will notice.

Chapter 4

Jessica walked into class.
Willy Cook laughed
and pointed at her hat.
"Hey, Jessica," he said.
"Are you going
to the beach today?"

26

"Please take your seats,"

said Mr. Ramos.

"The heater is not working well,

so keep on your coats.

And your hats."

Whew! thought Jessica.

"Here is my half
of our report," said Sam.
"See, I wrote it neatly.
Now it will be easy
for you to read to the class."
Oh, no! thought Jessica.
We have to give our report
after lunch. I forgot!

Jessica got out a pencil

and a piece of paper.

Can't talk, she wrote.

Sam's eyes got big.

"But you have to," he said.

"Why can't you?"

Jessica just pointed

to the words on the paper.

"I can't read

in front of the class,"

said Sam.

"I will get sick.

But if we don't

give our report — "

Jessica slid down in her seat.

What more can go wrong?

she worried.

Chapter 5

After recess, Mr. Ramos said,

"The room is warm now.

You may all take off your coats

and hats and hang them up."

Jessica hung up her coat.

She frowned.

What should I do about my hat?
she wondered.

Jessica went back

to her seat.

"Jessica," said Mr. Ramos,

"you didn't take off your hat."

Jessica did not move.

Mr. Ramos came closer.

What is he going to do?

thought Jessica.

"Is there a reason,"

Mr. Ramos asked,

"why you can't

take off your hat?"

Everyone looked at Jessica.

34

Jessica did not move.

Mr. Ramos frowned.

"Go to the principal's office,"
he said.

"I will come at lunchtime.
We will talk then."

Chapter 6

Jessica sat

in the principal's office.

What am I going to do?

she wondered.

How can I face Mr. Ramos

without a face?

Then the door opened.

Jessica stared.

Oh, no! she thought.

It's not Mr. Ramos.

It's Mom!

Jessica leaned back in her chair.

She tried to make herself

very small.

"Hi, Miss Bell," said Mrs. Jacobs
to the school secretary.
"I have something for Jessica.
May I go to her classroom?"
"Yes," said Miss Bell,
"but Jessica is here."

Mrs. Jacobs turned.

Her mouth fell open.

Then she smiled.

"I think you need this," she said.

Mrs. Jacobs gave Jessica

a brown paper bag.

Jessica took the big bag.

It was too heavy to be her lunch.

She looked inside the bag.

There was her head!

Jessica pulled it

out of the bag right away.

Then she remembered Miss Bell.

What will Miss Bell say?

Jessica worried.

Will she faint?

Jessica looked up.

Miss Bell was smiling.

"This happens to at least

one third grader every year,"

Miss Bell said.

Jessica put on her head.

"Thanks, Mom," she said.

"I wish you had told me
about this," said Mrs. Jacobs.

"I was afraid you would be mad,"
said Jessica.

Mrs. Jacobs smiled.

"Maybe," she said.

"But I love you.

And I will always help you

if I can. So please ask next time."

Jessica nodded a big nod.

Then Jessica remembered
the invitation to Sam's party.
She pulled it out of her pocket
and gave it to her mother.

"Jessica," said Mrs. Jacobs,

"this party is tonight!"

"I know," said Jessica.

"I'm sorry. I forgot to tell you."

Mrs. Jacobs shook her head.

Then she smiled

and put her hand

on Jessica's shoulder.

"OK," she said.

"What gift would Sam like?"